# GLADIATOR BOY VS

## THE ULTIMATE EVIL

*Other GLADIATOR BOY titles to collect:*

1. A HERO'S QUEST
2. ESCAPE FROM EVIL
3. STOWAWAY SLAVES
4. THE REBELS' ASSAULT
5. RESCUE MISSION
6. THE BLADE OF FIRE
7. THE LIVING DEAD
8. THE RAGING TORRENT
9. THE THREE NINJAS
10. THE INSANE FURY
11. THE WHITE SNAKE
12. THE GOLEM ARMY
13. THE SCREAMING VOID
14. THE CLONE WARRIORS
15. THE ULTIMATE EVIL

# GLADIATOR BOY VS

## THE ULTIMATE EVIL

### DAVID GRIMSTONE

Hodder
Children's
Books

A division of Hachette Children's Books

# HOW MANY
# GLADIATOR BOY
## BOOKS DO YOU HAVE?

A HERO'S QUEST

ESCAPE FROM EVIL

STOWAWAY SLAVES

THE REBELS' ASSAULT

RESCUE MISSION

THE BLADE OF FIRE

DAVID GRIMSTONE

GLADIATOR BOY VS THE LIVING DEAD
DAVID GRIMSTONE

GLADIATOR BOY VS THE THREE NINJAS
DAVID GRIMSTONE

GLADIATOR BOY VS THE RAGING TORRENT
DAVID GRIMSTONE

GLADIATOR BOY VS THE INSANE FURY
DAVID GRIMSTONE

GLADIATOR BOY VS THE GOLEM ARMY
DAVID GRIMSTONE

GLADIATOR BOY VS THE WHITE SNAKE
DAVID GRIMSTONE

# ITALY

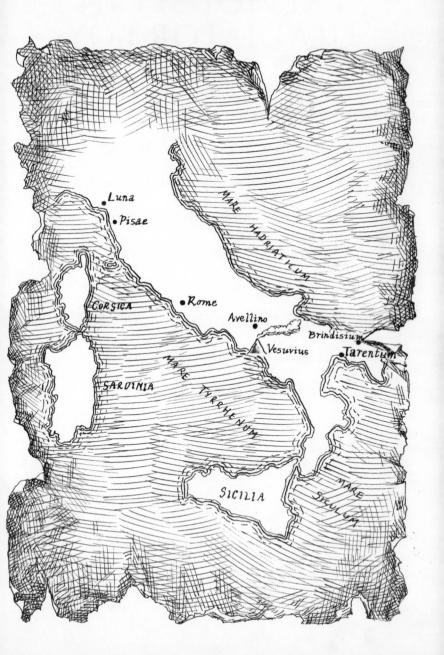

# PREVIOUSLY IN GLADIATOR BOY

Leaving Decimus and his friends to die at the hands of the Mirror Master's strange and sickening clones, Slavious Doom has snatched the boy's parents and is planning to throw them into the mouth of Mount Vesuvius. However, a whirlwind of anger is rising in his wake. While Decimus and Argon go in search of the lost Blade of Fire, the remaining slaves have freed more than two hundred children, all of whom are eager to have their revenge upon the evil overlord and end his reign of terror ... permanently.

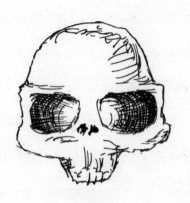

# CHAPTER
I

# THE
RETURN
TO
PRIMUS

'It's so much worse than I thought.'

Decimus peered over the ridge and looked down at the valley that had once contained the dreaded Arena of Doom. Now, all that remained of the great and terrible building was a massive pile of rubble that stretched as far as the eye could see in every direction. From the way rocks were strewn around the edge of the valley, it looked as if the arena had mostly collapsed outwards, though Decimus could definitely remember wandering through the tunnels beneath, feeling as though the place was caving *in* above him.

'Look,' Argon whispered, pointing down at a wide and tall section of rubble that had presumably been the very centre of Arena Primus. 'Doom's men are *still* here.'

Sure enough, it was true. An entire legion of
the overlord's soldiers was wading through the
debris in one part of the ruin, while teams of
guards in another shifted heavy blocks of stone
into piles.

'Do you think they're rebuilding the place?'
the Gaul continued. 'It certainly looks like

there's some sort of mission to—'

'They're looking for the Blade of Fire,' said Decimus, a grim assurance in his voice. 'Doom still desperately wants it, and wouldn't forget about it just to get his revenge upon *me*.'

The young gladiator turned to his friend with a sly smile. 'They won't find it, though. When the Maw swallowed it and sank into the depths of the earth, a thousand tons of rubble collapsed on top of the thing. It's going to take them years even to get through the *top* layer.'

Argon frowned.

'Then how are we supposed to find it?' he ventured.

'Because we know something they don't. We walked no more than six or seven tunnels in order to get out before the arena collapsed.

Sure, they were steep and really difficult to get through . . . but we still survived, and when we emerged into daylight, we weren't anywhere near where they're digging.' Decimus turned slightly and pointed toward the far end of the valley, at a barely visible pile of outlying rubble. 'We were over there.'

Argon allowed his gaze to follow his friend's pointed finger, and beamed an equally sly smile. 'So we were!'

'Let's go.'

The two companions hurried around the top of the ridge and swiftly navigated the higher foothills that sloped down to the valley floor, picking their way carefully through clearings that might have been visible to the soldiers far below.

Staying out of sight in the lower hills, Decimus and Argon found their way to the outlying rubble in no time at all, and immediately began to shift some of the smaller rocks blocking a patch of ground that Decimus was sure covered the exit they'd come through on that fateful day, two years before.

An hour passed in the sweltering sunlight, but the heavy, exhausting labour bore no fruit . . . and still there were more rocks.

After a second hour, however, Argon suddenly hefted aside a massive rock and stopped dead.

'Here!' he said, almost jumping up and down with glee. 'There's a hole right here!'

Decimus joined his friend. Sure enough, there was an opening visible beneath the stones, just large enough to accommodate one of them at a time.

'What are we waiting for?' Argon said, wriggling down into the hole before Decimus could even muster a reply.

The young gladiator took one last glance toward the distant soldiers, and followed.

The tunnel was hot and impossibly dark,

with only a sliver of light from the hole to illuminate their passage.

'We're going to need a torch,' Argon muttered as he almost tripped over a stack of rocks that were blocking the path.

Decimus shook his head. 'No, we can't afford to waste any more time messing about,' he said. 'The Maw's cavern had a natural green light that swelled up from the beast itself. As soon as we get close we should be able to see ... if it's still alive.'

Argon gasped in the darkness. 'You're not serious?' he muttered. 'How do you expect to find your way back to the cavern in the pitch dark? It's *impossible.*'

Decimus moved past the Gaul and patted his friend companionably on the shoulder.

'Nothing's impossible,' he said. 'Besides, I remember these tunnels from the escape. I don't know why; maybe, deep down, I had a feeling I'd be back here, someday. Hell, maybe the prophecy *is* right.'

He marched on ahead, leaving Argon walking despondently after him.

Gladius reached the lip of the track he'd been following and held up a large, podgy hand. The mass of former slaves gathered behind him suddenly shuffled to a halt, but this happened slowly, as the various other groups led by Teo, Olu and Ruma also came to a standstill. They were all armed with swords stolen from the Mirror Master's subterranean fortress, so the general slowing of their progress was anything but silent.

Ruma, always one to question any decision he hadn't actually made himself, hurried up to the big slave to see what was going on.

'Gladius,' he said briskly, noticing they were now looking out over a broad spread of what passed in the region for country farmland. 'Why have we stopped?'

'We're getting too close.'

'To Doom? Surely that's a good thing!'

Gladius shook his head.

'We don't want a confrontation before he gets to the mountain. Decimus should be the first to—'

'Are you mad?' Olu, who had been approaching and had overheard the conversation, looked shocked. 'Surely we want to stop him from ever *reaching* Mount Vesuvius? Are we planning to wait until Decimus's mum and dad are actually thrown into the volcano before we attack?'

The big slave sighed.

'Of course not, but we don't want to waste our only chance to defeat Doom and his army. Don't forget the Mirror Master is *with* him, and he's supposed to be a genius, right? I seriously doubt we can defeat Doom, all his men *and* the Mirror Master without Decimus and Argon behind us.'

Ruma looked suddenly disgusted.

'We have an entire *army*,' he whined.

'Exactly,' said Gladius, nodding. 'And we don't want to waste them by sacrificing them on the altar of our *own* stupidity. So we should continue to follow Doom *at a steady pace* until we reach the volcano. If Decimus *still* hasn't shown up by then,

we make our move. Agreed?'

Ruma and Olu paused for a moment, and then both gave a reluctant nod.

Finally, Teo arrived beside the group.

'What I miss?' he said, causing the others to burst out laughing.

Decimus was feeling his way along the tunnel system in total darkness, edging forward so carefully that anyone capable of observing him would have thought he was on the edge of a cliff. Argon followed along behind him, listening for the sound of his voice.

So far, they had encountered and removed three different obstructions, all of collapsed stone and all blocking the tunnel from floor to ceiling. Two had taken mere minutes to shift, but the last one had drained the pair of both time and effort. Now, they were both fairly exhausted.

'It's not much further until this tunnel hits a junction,' Decimus assured his friend, as the floor suddenly sloped at a sharp angle.

'I still can't understand how you remember this place so well,' Argon mumbled. 'It was all a blur to me; we were running *so* fast.'

'This way.' Decimus continued along the passage, before his voice suddenly changed and seemed to come from another direction. 'I've gone right at the divide – try to feel the breeze on your face – it's coming from the main cavern.'

Argon followed, sliding around the bend in the passage.

Down.

Down.

Dowwwwn.

After what felt like an age, Argon began to notice Decimus's bold outline up ahead of him. The revealed sight could mean only one thing – the glow from the Maw was still alight, and reached this far into the complex. It would be easier from here on in.

'I don't understand why we can't hear anything,' Decimus observed, quickening his pace. 'I remember that roar as if it started inside my own ears.'

Argon shrugged. 'Maybe it's sleeping.'

'We can hope.'

The glow was now clearly visible, a greenish wash that seemed to shift and travel over the tunnel roof as though in some bizarre dance of light.

The two boys doubled their efforts, sprinting along each new tunnel with renewed determination. As they proceeded deeper and deeper into the subterranean network, the glowing light grew stronger and stronger, developing from a wash to an all-out beam of emerald intensity.

At length, Decimus rounded one final bend in the last passage, and skidded to an unexpected and rather abrupt halt.

Argon cannoned into him, and the pair almost tumbled down the collapsed underground canyon that now spread out before them.

'Look!' Decimus gasped. 'In the name of the gods – it's even bigger than I remembered!'

Argon said nothing: he couldn't agree with his friend more, but his mouth simply refused to open.

Ahead of them and far below was a vast, meandering crack in the earth. Above ground, it would have looked like a vast chasm,

impossibly deep and unthinkably wide. Here, however, it just looked like a gap in the floor, or a crack in a line of plaster.

The main reason for this was the Maw, an octopus-like beast so far beyond size as to be almost unimaginable. It was half in and half out of the gap, like a bloated spider hiding inside a wall-crevice with only its legs spilling out above the surface.

Decimus swallowed, suddenly realizing the enormous task ahead of him. Currently, the hideous expanse of the Maw's countless eyes was nowhere to be seen, presumably because the beast was either dead or sleeping. Decimus suspected the latter, as a terrible shuddering rhythm suggested it was not only alive but still, inconceivably, well.

'I thought you killed it!' Argon whispered in his ear, finally finding a shaky voice in the horrible cavern.

Decimus shook his head. 'I knew it wasn't dead,' he muttered. 'I'm just shocked it survived the collapse so ... well ... intact. Now listen to me, Argon – I need you to climb up to that top ridge and start screaming, as loud as you can for as *long* as you can. When the beast awakes and starts extending its tentacles, you're going to need to run *around* the ridge, avoiding them. I chose you to come with me because you're the only one strong enough to have a chance of breaking free if it *does* get hold of you. Now, did you get all that?'

Argon nodded, but looked momentarily puzzled. 'What are you going to be doing, exactly?'

Decimus grinned. 'Don't ask!'

He edged forward slightly, holding on to the rocks at either side of the tunnel mouth.

'Well,' he whispered. 'Here goes nothing.'

With that, he slid down the wall to the valley floor, and began sneaking carefully towards the sleeping monster.

# CHAPTER
## II

# INTO
# THE
# MAW

*S*lavious Doom felt the approach of his apprentice even before the man drew near to him. There was something ever so slightly uncomfortable about Islaw Danis, the man who preferred himself to be called the Mirror Master.

'Is there a problem?' Doom asked, before the long-haired warrior had even announced his presence.

If Danis jumped even slightly, he did not show it. Instead, he glanced over his shoulder at the long line of soldiers ... and at the two slaves they were dragging in their wake.

'Not a problem exactly, my lord,' said Danis, edging closer still and lowering his voice. 'Rex's parents are being given water every few hours, so all is fine there. We should reach the volcano in a little under two hours, in fact.'

Doom raised a dark eyebrow. 'Well then? To what do I owe your sudden company?'

His apprentice paused again, as if he was frightened to make any further comment. Then, very suddenly, his confidence seemed to increase.

'I wonder about the wisdom of the decision you made back at the fortress, my lord.'

'Oh?' Doom smiled to himself: he'd predicted this exact conversation.

'Well, it's just that if Decimus Rex is such a powerful warrior – was it entirely, um, sensible to leave him and his companions to fight the Specials *unobserved*? I mean, I have every faith in my creations, but it's just on the edge of possibility that ...'

'... that Decimus and his friends overcame them and escaped?'

Doom turned his great head slightly and his eyes narrowed to mere slits. 'And then overcame the vile Captain Lich and his men, releasing all the child slaves from the wall at the same time?'

The Mirror Master was speechless. All he

managed was a weak and trembling nod.

'I expect you are right,' Doom finished. 'And that even now those pathetic rascals are building an army in the hope of saving that pair of ageing peasants behind me?'

The Mirror Master finally found his voice.

'Y-yes, my lord – but if . . .'

'. . . if I know all this, why am I doing nothing? It's really quite simple.' Doom cackled as he strode along. 'Decimus Rex will not come after me unarmed, not this time – he knows I survived his last attack and will never again underestimate my strength. No, in order to save his parents, he will take his new army in search of the one thing he thinks he needs in order to defeat me.'

A sudden realization dawned on the Mirror

Master's stunned face.

'The Blade of Fire!' he exclaimed.

'Exactly.' Doom turned to his apprentice with an evil, knowing smile. 'And I would hazard a guess that, even as we speak, my young friend and his horde of young warriors are doing everything they can to get it back . . . *exactly* as I had planned. Relax, Islaw – it will take Decimus and his army *many* days to reach us . . . and be assured that we will be ready for them when they do.'

The Mirror Master grinned at the overlord's intricate plan, but he couldn't help but feel slightly uneasy: *he was secretly quite certain that they were being closely followed.*

Argon could feel his heart pounding in his chest. Every muscle straining with effort, he dragged himself over the edge of the ridge and on to the narrow, circular path that ran around the boundary of the cavern roof.

Leaping to his feet, Argon peered down at the distant floor, trying to see where Decimus had gone ... but there was no sign of his friend.

Swallowing a few times and trying to stop himself shaking, Argon took a deep breath and held it for several seconds. Then he let out the most powerful, booming yell he'd ever uttered.

The high-pitched cry echoed all around the cavern, bouncing from every crevice in the pitted roof and gathering more reverberations even as it died away.

Down in the base of the cavern, the Maw

twitched so thunderously that a great column of rock collapsed as the tentacles flashed back and forth. The great, jet black, slime-encrusted body of the beast began to emerge from its hole, looking even more like a fat and hairy spider as the tentacles dragged its bulk upwards. All at once, the many and gelatinous eyes of the *thing* sprang open in a terrible glare.

Argon began to run, slowly at first but gradually picking up the pace as the great beast began to move.

Then it happened.

Amid a colossal drive to leave its nest, the Maw gave a sudden, lurching shudder and then seemed to fall again, its tentacles scrambling madly on the cavern floor as it receded back into the hole.

*It's stuck*, Argon thought, suddenly pausing in his mad dash around the cavern perimeter.

*That's why it didn't break free after the collapse – it's actually stuck in the hole.*

He was about to relax when the tentacles

suddenly snapped out again, snaking high into the air and whipping around the walls in a mad frenzy.

Argon gasped and leapt aside, just as one of the Maw's giant limbs smashed a hole in the path where he'd been standing. This caused a small rock collapse that, Argon realized, might present some problems when he came around for his second circuit of the cavern.

Bellowing again, even *louder* this time, he continued his breakneck run, skidding to a halt when a second tentacle slammed into the wall ahead of him.

The Maw was evidently becoming extremely frustrated. It twitched, writhed and wriggled helplessly in the ground, its great twisting limbs searching for anything it could grip that would enable it to drag itself up and out of its rocky prison.

Unable to achieve this after several attempts, the beast's movements became more frantic. One tentacle flashed back and forth faster and faster, searching, probing, smashing away great sections of the walls. Then, in a raging torrent of frustration, it opened its massive, needle-filled jaws and roared with such deafening ferocity that the entire cavern shook in a great quake.

As the Maw's mouth widened and stretched to the limits of its physical capability, Decimus appeared from behind a collapsed section of rock on the cavern floor and – to Argon's astonishment – leapt over two of the tentacles as he hurtled *towards* the central mass of the Maw.

Then, taking a giant and apparently suicidal leap, the young gladiator dived directly between the jaws of the beast, disappearing inside it as they snapped shut in a sudden, reactive gulp.

Argon froze, mid-yell, too stunned by the sight even to continue with his friend's plan.

Decimus had been consumed by the Maw . . . and he'd done it *on purpose*.

The army of Slavious Doom climbed Mount Vesuvius in three separate groups. The first, led by the overlord himself and his deceptively agile apprentice, were nearly at the crater. The second group, comprising the main mass of the army, were still a little way behind them. The last group were a good distance away, still dragging the parents of Decimus Rex through the mud and pausing every few hours to punish the pair in small and malicious ways for slowing them down.

As the crater of Vesuvius came into sight, Doom turned to the Mirror Master with a grave expression on his craggy face.

'We will camp on the edge of the crater for a few days, to give our young friend enough time to find and retrieve the sword.'

The Mirror Master shook his head. 'You really think he...'

'...absolutely. He is *destined* to possess it... and when he does – when he and his friends attack – I want you and the men to separate him from the others. Do you understand? I want to fight Decimus Rex *alone*.'

The Mirror Master bowed slightly. 'As you wish, my lord.'

Decimus Rex's friends strongly suspected that he was incapable of feeling *fear*. In fact, the opposite was true: Decimus had been terrified in the face of every opponent, every trap and every danger he had ever faced. The thing that made him look so fearless to his friends was the fact that he had learned to channel all his terror and use it to his own advantage. This occasion was no different: he felt the fear building inside him . . . and began to turn it around.

The incredible, needle-thin jaws of the Maw slammed shut above him and he landed with a

wet plop on something that he just knew,

instinctively, had to be the monster's lolling

tongue. The slimy surface, which convulsed

reactively upon his landing, contained what felt

like hundreds and hundreds of tiny hairs. They

impeded his progress, for as the Maw's tongue

made every effort to flip him into its massive

throat, the hairs were halting his downward slide. Decimus fought them, wrenching his arms and legs away from the carpet of tiny spikes in an attempt to force himself into a further dive for the beast's stomach.

It worked.

Decimus peeled himself away from the huge, lolling tongue and slid vertically down the tunnel of the Maw's pulsating throat. Down he plunged, faster and faster, assisting his passage by keeping his arms and legs tight together.

The horrible tract he found himself in flashed by in a blur, and he plummeted through stinking rotten air for a fraction of a second before splashing into a tumultuous soup like a stone dropped into water. He sank beneath the surface, holding his breath as the tide of putrid liquid rose and fell above him.

Opening his eyes, he could barely see through the murky gloom of the Maw's foul stomach contents. On reflection, this was probably just as well: only the gods knew what such a creature would have devoured before its forced hibernation.

Then he saw the glow. Even in the inky swell of the stomach fluid, the blade shimmered and shone like a candle.

Decimus surfaced once again, took a deep gulp of the wretched air and dived below, propelling himself through the stomach pool and making for the blade with a grim determination.

The Maw was going crazy.

Argon had been forced to hurtle around the cavern ridge at breakneck speed, leaping increasingly bigger and bigger gaps as the beast's raging tentacles blasted more and more of the rocky path away.

Still bellowing with every breath he had left, Argon kept up the pace, feeling his energy beginning to ebb away from him, until finally ... he collapsed on to his knees. Puffing and panting out great lungfuls of air, Argon could only look on helplessly, as his greatest fears came to life, right before his eyes.

Two of the probing, thrashing tentacles finally found their way to the tunnels at either end of the cavern roof, and snaked inside. After a few, frantic seconds, they pulled taut, dragging the bodily mass of the Maw with far greater intensity.

It took only three great heaves before the beast began to escape. Argon looked on, petrified, as more and more of the gigantic monster's great bulk became visible, squeezing itself from the crack as its great feelers wrenched it upwards.

Then, all at once, the Maw was free.

Tentacles now lifting as well as pulling its enormous frame, the beast scrambled across the cavern floor, convulsing as if caught in some inner struggle. Its jaws snapped back and forth as its eyes searched the area madly for the source of the screaming that had awoken it.

The Maw's nest of emerald eyeballs darted about until they fixed upon the hunched form of Argon, still on his knees atop the ridge pathway.

Moving at a speed that seemed impossible for a creature of such size, the Maw made its way up the cavern walls. Argon could only stare at his approaching nemesis. The beast looked like the giant, mutated offspring of a spider and an octopus as it lashed out a stream of its deadly tentacles.

Argon closed his eyes as the giant feelers came smashing down, and tried to pray to the gods to take him quickly.

There was a terrible rush of air.

The Maw screamed ... and it *was* a scream. Unlike the terrible, shuddering roar that had rocked the cavern earlier, this high-pitched, wailing cry was akin to the sound a thousand wounded dogs might make if they all howled at the same time. It was absolutely deafening and

Argon, suddenly aware that he was still alive and breathing, raised two hands to cover his ears. When a second scream rocked the cavern, he slowly chanced opening his eyes in order to see what was happening.

The Maw had fallen from the ridge path, and

was writhing around on the cavern floor, its tentacles flailing madly in the air.

For a second, Argon just stared down at the beast, wide-eyed, completely unsure of exactly what was happening to it.

Then the sword appeared. The fiery, glowing blade erupted from the stomach of the beast in one swift thrust, spewing a fountain of green liquid all over the floor of the cavern.

The blade cut downwards, opening a neat line in the Maw's slimy flesh as it continued to scream. Its tentacles suddenly withdrew as if to scratch an infuriating itch.

Decimus exploded from the belly of the beast, bursting forth on the wave of rank stomach juice that gushed from within.

Sliding across the cavern floor, Decimus

quickly flipped himself over and scrambled on to his feet, just as the Maw made a furious, desperate lunge for him with all eight of its tentacles.

Now screaming with an intensity that put Argon's former cries to shame, the giant feelers whipped around in a series of wild arcs as they prepared for a final, devastating attack.

Decimus had a face like black thunder. Moving to stand on firmer, rockier ground, he crouched in a battle stance, clutching the Blade of Fire in both hands, his eyes narrowed to slits as he watched the movement of every tentacle with acute awareness.

Two of the giant feelers shot out for the attack, but Decimus moved like a flash of lightning. The young gladiator hacked off the end of the first tentacle in one sweeping cut and promptly leapt over the next, only to dash after it and slice the end cleanly away.

Another series of howling screams echoed around the cavern, as streams of the green liquid vaulted from the tips of the wounded feelers. The other tentacles were quickly withdrawn in a wild panic.

Giving the beast no opportunity to regroup for a new attack, Decimus spun the glowing blade around in a full circle and hurtled towards the main body of the Maw.

Watching from the ridge above, Argon felt cold and useless. He just stood, in a state of bewildered awe, as his friend ploughed into the shuddering mass, driving the blade forward in a frenzy of demented thrusts and sending up great sprays of the jade-coloured blood in every direction.

Finally, the Maw gave one last, ear-splitting, ground-shuddering roar of despair . . . before its mass visibly deflated. The remaining tentacles flopped lifelessly on the cavern floor and trembled slightly, the movement slowly easing as the life left them.

Decimus staggered back from the enormous mass of the beast and collapsed on to his knees, the sword clattering to his side. As Argon half slipped, half tumbled down the rocky walls of the cavern, Decimus began to wretch as his body threw up the filthy soup he had swallowed in the stinking stomach of the Maw. Despite the horrible sickness and the urge to cleanse his system of the filthy liquid, Decimus allowed himself an exhausted smile.

The first battle was over: the Blade of Fire had finally been retrieved.

'Here he comes.'

Gladius grinned at the approaching shape of Teo, who was dashing along the side of the volcano at such a high speed that even Ruma and Olu couldn't watch without passing a remark on it. The little slave had been sent off to scout out the crater, while the rest of the army rested on the far side of the mountain. It was a good plan to use Teo, who was so stealthy that he could probably have sneaked past even the most keen-eyed observer in *plain sight*.

However, the puzzled look on the little

slave's face didn't exactly fill the others with confidence.

'They make camp,' Teo said, pausing to draw breath as he reached the group. 'Top of mountain; some sleeping now.'

'Why would they put down a camp?' Ruma exclaimed, his eyes searching Gladius's face for any sign of an answer. 'It doesn't make sense.'

'I agree,' added Olu. 'Why not just throw Decimus's parents into the crater if that's what he's come here to do.'

'"If that's what he's come here to do",' Gladius said, repeating the other slave's words almost as if he didn't realize he was speaking aloud. 'But … but what if killing Decimus's family *isn't* the thing he's come here to do?'

The statement provoked confused expressions

from Olu, Ruma and Teo, but Gladius continued following his own thoughts to their conclusion.

'Don't get me wrong,' he muttered. 'I'm certain Doom means to execute them, but what if that's not his *main* reason for coming here? Remember, he left the arena *before* we defeated the Specials – entrusting them to finish us off completely unobserved. Doom is not usually so careless.'

Ruma and Olu shared a glance. 'So what does that mean exactly?'

'A camp indicates that he's waiting for something,' said Gladius, scratching his head. 'And considering volcanic eruptions are completely unpredictable ... my guess is that he's waiting for us.'

'Us?' Olu gawked at him. 'But that's ridiculous – are you saying that everything we've been through, from escaping the glass fortress and freeing the slaves to this *insane* journey, was *planned* by Doom as a trap?'

Gladius nodded, but it was Ruma who spoke.

'Not a trap for us,' he muttered. 'A trap for Decimus: I suspect Doom thinks Decimus is with us and that we are all still some way behind him. For once, I would disagree with you, Gladius – those men up there are camping because they do *not* expect an immediate attack. For whatever reason, Doom thinks we are all *somewhere else*. That is why I strongly suggest that we strike now, in the cover of darkness ... and catch them all unaware.'

Gladius thought for a moment, and then

nodded. 'You're right,' he said, pointing to Teo.
'But I think we should we attack with stealth,
not frenzy.'

# CHAPTER III

# MIDNIGHT AMBUSH

Decimus raced along the tunnels, holding aloft the Blade of Fire to light his path. The orange glow bathed the passage in a wash of pale light, illuminating the bedraggled form of Argon, who was still exhausted from his mad dash around the cavern.

'Vesuvius is more than a day away,' Decimus shouted, turning right down a new passage that, thankfully, began to slope upwards. 'We'll cut directly across the hills, but we still can't slow

down and make camp until we're at least in sight of the mountain.'

He put his head down and ran on, guided by both the flame and the distant, hopeful prospect of fresh air.

Midnight arrived.

The crater of Mount Vesuvius was smoking, but not because the volcano was about to erupt. The particular flames currently burning all over

the top of the mountain were man-made, as various groups of soldiers gathered around a variety of temporary cooking fires. Many of the men were already asleep, leaving a skeleton crew to take the first shift of the evening.

In one corner of the crater, a team of brutish-looking thugs watched over Decimus's terrified parents, though their attention to the wretched pair didn't extend to offering them any of the food they were cooking.

Near the edge of the crater, Doom and the Mirror Master were locked in some sort of in-depth discussion with three of the army commanders. Occasionally, Doom would mutter something that caused the senior officers to roar with laughter, but it was the enforced merriment of fear rather than any genuine appreciation of the overlord's good humour.

Only the Mirror Master looked distracted from the conversation. The long-haired, noble-faced warrior kept darting concerned glances left and right, peering around the crater as if he was observing some strange, unseen enemy.

Unfortunately for the gathered army, Islaw Danis was looking in the opposite direction when the ambush actually took place.

Far from the sudden, roaring charge that Ruma would have had the slaves make, Gladius's planned attack was quite different.

Some fifty or sixty slaves poured over the perimeter of the crater, creeping in towards the sleeping soldiers on the edge of the camp with careful, deliberate movements. Their swords were drawn silently, and raised with equal discretion as the first wave of slaves crouched beside their unsuspecting foes.

Then, two things happened with such incredible speed that *no single* member of Doom's army had enough time to muster any sort of strong defence.

First, the stealthy invaders slayed the sleeping guards with comparative ease. Secondly, the remaining legion of slaves came charging over the lip of the crater with a combined scream of rage so terrifying that it literally threw the whole of Doom's army into a mad, wild panic.

All over the sides of the crater, armoured soldiers clashed with young slaves dressed in mere rags of cloth. However, the vast physical differences between the boys and their former tormentors were easily outweighed by the ferocity with which they fought: every slave desperately wanted vengeance, while the soldiers merely defended themselves in the same way they would have done against any other enemy. Passion was carrying the battle, and it was swinging every clash in favour of the slave army.

Slavious Doom clambered to his feet, drawing his great sword from its demon-crested scabbard and swinging it around in readiness for the first attack. Beside him, the Mirror Master also leapt up, but he produced not one but two thin swords from a sling-pack across his back, swinging them both in a complicated series of arcs as he moved to his master's side.

However, Doom had frozen to the spot. The overlord's face was a mask of sudden confusion, and he couldn't hide his surprise at the sight of his newly arrived attackers. As his eyes searched the line of foes, he saw no sign of Decimus Rex: none whatsoever.

All he saw before him were the determined faces of Gladius, Olu, Teo and Ruma: the four young friends of his arch enemy screamed a raging battle cry ... and hurtled towards him. Doom roared his own bellowing threat, and leapt forward to meet them, Danis close at his heels.

Night yawned over the hills west of the arena, as Decimus and Argon camped beside a flickering fire. The Gaul had fallen into a deep sleep, but Decimus knew they couldn't rest for too long. They still had a long way to go.

Suppressing a wide yawn, the young gladiator felt himself begin to nod off, but managed to avoid the ravages of sleep by rubbing his eyelids with his rough fingers.

As he sat by the edge of the fire, silently yawning, his tired gaze briefly settled on the glowing Blade of Fire which was propped against the rock beside him. He reached out to touch the weapon, but his clumsy grasp only caused it to slide off the rock and clatter loudly to the ground.

Decimus looked over at Argon, but the Gaul began to snore, showing no sign that his own rest had been disturbed by the noise.

It was only when Decimus leaned over to retrieve the weapon that he noticed something had been knocked out of place: the pommel was slightly apart from the hilt. He reached out and picked up the sword, turning it upside down in order to get a closer look at the damage.

In fact, it wasn't damage at all. Pulling at the pommel, he discovered a small, concealed space inside the hilt. Working his fingers into the narrow hole, he felt a tiny roll of parchment, and quickly dragged it out of its hiding place.

The parchment looked old beyond any count of years, and almost fell apart as Decimus rolled it open. Slowly, his lips muttering and mumbling as he went, Decimus began to read about the long and terrible history of the weapon he was holding.

When he'd finished reading, the young gladiator's eyes were drawn to the sword. He found his gaze fixed on the pulsating glow of the blade, and his eyes were filled with tears.

The two armies clashed violently all over the crater. Hordes of screaming children, armed with swords and fired up with the determination of revenge, broke against the wall of soldiers like a giant wave crashing over lines of jagged rocks.

However, despite the incredible ferocity of the attack, a single fact remained: the soldiers were trained to fight, and their smaller opponents were not. Without the lion roar of a determined and heroic leader, the youthful army of the tortured and persecuted slaves could only hold back the mass of soldiers and seemed unable to do any significant damage to their opponent's numbers.

The quartet of warriors who should have been leading them were otherwise engaged, wrapped up in a pitched battle of their own on the far side of the crater.

Slavious Doom smirked at Ruma and Gladius as the pair approached him. Maintaining his battle stance, he neither flinched nor averted his gaze when the first sword was thrust forward.

Doom blocked Gladius's clumsy lunge and swung his incredible bulk around to blast Ruma aside before the skinny Etrurian could muster a single strike. Then he blocked a second, more calculated lunge from the big slave, delivering a forearm blow which drove the boy backwards and knocked the wind from his lungs. Two swords clattered on to the ground, only to be snatched up again as the frustrated slaves groped around in panic.

'Pathetic,' Doom growled. 'I needn't have bothered unsheathing my blade.'

Across from him, Islaw Danis was making short work of both Teo and Olu. The smallest, quickest member of the slave group had attacked the Mirror Master head on, relying on his greater stealth to carry him through the combat. Only, as it turned out, Teo didn't *have* greater stealth than the Mirror Master: the long-haired warrior outpaced him at every turn, eventually disarming him and thrusting one of his two blades deep into the small boy's shoulder. Teo cried out, and staggered back, but Olu's attempt to save his friend had an even more disastrous result.

The gangly slave, who had already tried and failed several times to work his own sword through the Mirror Master's incredible defences, made a frantic thrust in order to block Danis's obvious attempt to finish Teo off.

The Mirror Master did something both unpredictable and completely unexpected with his two swords: he threw them into the air. Wrong-footed by the move, Olu inexplicably found his gaze following the trajectory of the blades. When, in the split second that he realized his mistake, he shook himself out of the reverie and drove his own weapon forward, the Mirror Master caught the two swords and twisted them into a sharp cross, snapping Olu's blade in half.

The lanky slave gasped, looked down at his broken sword, and was sent crashing to the ground by single, high kick to the chest.

Olu quickly rolled over on to his stomach, and screamed. In the few seconds it had taken him to move, Islaw Danis was upon him. With a single demonic thrust, he drove the blade into Olu's back, just below the shoulder.

The gangly slave cried out again, and writhed around in agony.

'You are both wounded in the same way,' Danis said, in a calm voice, looking down at the two fallen boys. 'Neither of you will die, but you will be disabled for a short time . . . at least until all your friends have been defeated. Now, please excuse me – I must assist my master.'

Doom was almost disappointed with his opponents. He'd always known that Gladius would be no physical match for him, but he'd expected a good deal more from Ruma. The scrawny Etrurian, whom Doom had always considered second only to Decimus in the combat stakes, was either completely intimidated or exceptionally tired. Doom reflected that it was probably both, yet still he showed no mercy.

Slamming a fist into the side of Gladius's head and kicking the big slave's legs out from under him, he took a few seconds to step back and admire his handiwork, spinning at the last second to block Ruma's incoming sword strike with a single sweep of his own giant blade. The weapons met with a heavy clash, but the Etrurian's sword flew wide, taking him with it.

Doom laughed with undisguised glee as he followed up on the strike.

Ruma hit the ground with a thud, yet managed to keep hold of his sword and immediately struck back, swinging an arc of steel at Doom's legs. The overlord leapt into the air, cleanly evading the thrust, but evidently forgetting about Gladius, who returned at that moment with a punch that actually knocked Doom slightly off guard.

The overlord rallied with incredible speed, however, swinging back with a punch that knocked the big slave unconscious. He landed with a spine-juddering crash on top of Ruma, who physically convulsed on impact.

Doom sprang to his feet, just as his wily apprentice arrived on the scene.

Danis wasted no time at all, dragging Ruma away from the overlord and pummelling him with a series of well-placed blows that left him disoriented and barely conscious.

Doom grinned at the resulting chaos, and stared out across the crater: his men were winning the combat. Many of the soldiers had simply disarmed the young slaves and were toying with them, allowing them to take their best shots before mercilessly slapping them down. Others were more forthright in their attacks, and were beating the children severely.

The attack had failed, and the advantage had been lost.

Decimus and Argon ran on through the early hours, using their renewed energy to close the already shrinking distance between them and the looming volcano.

Argon had found Decimus's story about the discovery of the scroll absolutely enthralling, but to his annoyance the young gladiator hadn't yet revealed what he'd learned by reading it.

'Can you tell me what the scroll said?' he panted.

Decimus puffed out his own breath of air. 'I'd always heard that the Blade of Fire glowed with an "unearthly flame",' he said, pacing himself, 'and that the gods made it as a weapon of power for the strong and the good of the land to wield against evil. Now, however, I've learned the truth – it is a *cursed* weapon ... I don't think anyone alive today really knows that. Doom told me a long time ago that I bore the Mark of the Blade. See, here on my neck,' he indicated, slowing slightly. 'Legend told that the bearer of this mark was destined to retrieve the Blade of Fire. It seems that this is what Doom always wanted me for ... but he can't possibly know what I've just learned about the sword.'

'What exactly have you learned?' Argon asked, trying to keep the fear from his voice as he ran. 'I mean, how *is* the sword cursed?'

Decimus ran in silence for a time.

'The Blade of Fire was made by the god of

war,' he said, eventually. 'It simply brings death and destruction to all those who wield it. The legend in the scroll isn't exactly clear, but it seems that the gods had grown tired of the fighting of men – millions of years of wars and anger and death – so this weapon was a trick on the bloodthirsty. All who seek to kill another with it will die.'

'I think I understand,' Argon spluttered, as he hurried along beside the young gladiator. 'Basically, if you use it to kill, it is *you* who ends up slain.'

'No wonder it was hidden so well,' Decimus finished, grimacing slightly as he ran on. 'It's quite literally a double-edged sword.'

# CHAPTER
## IV

# DOOM

Morning yawned over the mouth of Mount Vesuvius, and the edge of the crater was a ravaged battleground. Although there were no actual corpses littering the ground, some of the young slaves had been beaten so badly that they lay just as still as if they'd been killed.

In one corner, a pile of swords represented the disarming of the slave army, while another was taken up by the mass of soldiers who now gathered eagerly for the spectacle that was about to unfold.

The Mirror Master, his face a mask of amusement, led a small group of soldiers towards a narrow jut of rock that spilled out over the crater. In front of the group, being urged forward by the swords in their backs,

were Gladius, Olu, Teo, Ruma and the parents
of Decimus Rex.

All six prisoners were driven on to the rock,
their expressions ranging from fear to despair.
Ruma's determination had left him, Teo and Olu
were ravaged and beaten, even Gladius found
himself at a loss to think of anything except the
terrible fate now awaiting them.

The group reached the very edge of the rock,
and Doom held up a hand, halting their
progress.

*Just a few more minutes*, he thought to himself.
*I can almost feel the boy approaching. If my plans have
worked perfectly, he will have the Blade with him . . .
and then it will be mine.*

He raised both hands to his mouth and cried
out across the crater: 'We are gathered here

today, to discover the dark destiny awaiting *any* and *all* who oppose my rule. You slaves, cowering in the dirt before me, be warned: you can follow these foolish children ... or you can follow me!'

Doom peered around the crater as he spoke, but there was no sign yet of Decimus Rex. Fortunately, he knew just how to kill time before he despatched the boy's parents.

He took a deep breath, and bellowed: 'Send the first one over!'

A series of sidelong glances

quickly informed the group that, of their number, Ruma was closest to the edge.

The wiry Etrurian felt the blade dig into his back, and took two small steps forward. Looking back at the tear-filled faces of his friends seemed to somehow restore his fighting spirit, and Ruma smiled, shouting at the top of his voice: 'Doom! The last time you had your idiots throw me from a great height, I survived!'

The overlord's face spread into a wide grin.

'I doubt you'll manage the same thing this time, you pathetic gnat,' he roared. 'Your days of escaping my wrath are over. Hahahahaha!'

Ruma swallowed, and felt himself begin to shake. Again, the sword bit into the flesh at the small of his back ... but this time he could think of no brave words to say. He simply nodded goodbye to the friends he loved, and stepped out over the drop.

'DOOOOOOOM!'

The voice resounded so powerfully that Ruma balked, and would have fallen into the volcano had Olu not steadied him.

Slavious Doom looked east, and saw two figures approaching. One was carrying a sword that glowed, even in the harsh light of day. A smile spread across Doom's dark features like treacle.

'Look, men!' the overlord boomed. 'Look and behold: the great Decimus Rex approaches!'

The army, almost as one, turned to view the scene. A short distance from the encampment, Argon suddenly stopped ... but the young gladiator continued to head straight for the rocky ridge that supported Slavious Doom.

'You see what I carry?' Decimus boomed, once again, holding the sword aloft.

Doom tried not to let his glee betray him. 'If it isn't the fabled Blade of Fire!' he yelled. 'Why, you must have wrenched it from the very jaws of the Maw itself!'

Decimus also smiled, but his was a grin of complete determination: a grin in the face of adversity. The expression baffled Gladius, Olu, Ruma and Teo, who could see no reason for the young gladiator to look *quite* so confident. After all, he had a strong blade . . . but he also faced a vast *army* of opponents.

Still, Decimus walked on.

'So what is the deal, my young friend?' Doom oozed. 'The lives of your parents and your friends in exchange for the Blade?'

Out of the corner of his eye, Decimus saw the Mirror Master detach himself from the slave group and begin to move around behind him. His swords were sheathed, but he was holding a chain of some sort.

*Perfect.*

Decimus grinned again, and stopped dead.

Then he tossed the sword on to the ground in front of him, and lowered himself on to his knees.

'The deal is that I have had enough of all this killing, my lord,' he said, peering up at Doom. 'So I give you this weapon and ask that you spare my life and the lives of my friends and parents in return.'

As gasps flew up from the gathered slaves, a

look of complete puzzlement consumed the overlord's smug face.

Decimus was kneeling before him, and had ripped his ragged shirt apart to reveal a section of his pale, scarred chest.

'I beg for your mercy, Doom,' he cried, an edge to his voice that even Gladius had never heard.

Doom thought for a moment, and then positively beamed with triumph.

Motioning to the Mirror Master to quicken his pace, he climbed down from the ridge and approached the young gladiator, taking extra care to watch the boy as he picked up the sword in both hands.

'I have it!' Doom screamed, practically crying out to the gods. 'At last, the Blade of Fire is mine! Hahaha!'

The Mirror Master moved behind Decimus and briskly looped the chain he was carrying around the boy's neck.

'Just being *sure*, master,' he growled.

Doom was so focused on the sword that he barely noticed the gesture, but he looked up and nodded some small thanks to his apprentice when his gaze finally returned to the boy.

Decimus knelt, awaiting Doom's mercy, his chest bared and his neck wrapped with the chain. He cast a last, hopeful glance at the overlord, and begged for his life.

'Please, Lord Doom, please ... I am sorry for the embarrassment I have caused you. Spare my life, and the lives of all those I love. I beg of you.'

Doom's fiery eyes locked with those of the boy at his mercy, and he smiled humourlessly.

'For all that you have done to me, Decimus Rex,' he growled, 'THIS is the mercy I give you.'

Doom rushed forward, and in a second that seemed to the slaves to last for an hour, drove his sword at the heart of Decimus Rex . . .

. . .

. . .

. . . but the boy wasn't there.

Moving with a snap reaction that would have been far beyond even Teo's quickest spring, Decimus twisted his entire body around and flung himself backwards with all his might. The chain around his neck was pulled forward with lightning speed and the sudden, dead weight of the young gladiator's entire body.

The Mirror Master, still clinging desperately to the end of the chain, flew forward like a bird, soaring into the air . . .

. . . just as Doom arced the Blade of Fire down
to where Decimus had been . . .

There was a second of

blurring chaos . . .

. . . and the sword plunged

into the Mirror Master's chest.

Silence.

Islaw Danis looked down, his

jaw dropping, and staggered

slightly. The sword embedded firmly in his chest, he looked up and smiled weakly at his master.

Then he fell.

Doom's face showed no more than a minor irritation as he strode up to his fallen companion in order to wrench free the sword for a second strike at the boy.

Then, all at once, the overlord seemed to feel an itch in his own chest.

Still reaching down for the blade, he put a hand to his armour, and released the front plate.

It clattered to the ground.

Doom looked down.

The slaves started to whoop, roar, and cheer their approval as the blood-red wash began to soak through Doom's tunic.

The overlord looked up, his eyes wild and

frantic, desperately searching for an answer as the life flowed from his veins.

'You want to know WHY?' Decimus shouted. The young gladiator was on his feet once again, and storming towards Doom.

The overlord sank to his knees.

'It's a *cursed* weapon,' the boy cried. 'Cursed to be wielded by men *just* like you: men who follow battle with battle, death with death.'

As Doom grasped the edge of Decimus's tunic and began to lose consciousness, the young gladiator snatched hold of his fallen nemesis and shouted: 'It's what you searched your whole life for, Doom . . . and now you're welcome to it.'

At the very last second, on the volcano crater, surrounded by once fearful minions and all those whom he had enslaved, the great and powerful

Slavious Doom met his fate.

As the evil overlord died, one by one his men dropped their weapons, some edging slowly away and others abandoning their confidence and simply running down the mountain.

Behind them, a roar started up at the crater top. It was a humming, thundering, rampaging cheer of

freedom, and it got louder ... and louder ... and louder ... and, though the voices of the many slaves gathered atop Vesuvius contributed to the vast sea of noise, none were louder and prouder than those of Olu, Ruma, Teo, Argon and Gladius: the freed heroes from the Arena of Doom.

Decimus Rex himself just smiled because he felt that his days of roaring were now *finally* over.

# GLADIATOR GAME

## THE TOURNAMENT!

This is an exciting game that can be played on your own or with friends. It is an elimination tournament, and features many of the characters from the Gladiator Boy saga. You will need two dice, some paper, a pencil, a bag or container and a number of counters or figures to represent each warrior! First, tear up twenty-one equally-sized pieces of paper and write the name of a character and the number you see next to that character (all listed below) on each one. The number represents the character's Life Points score: when this reaches 0, the character has been defeated and is out of the game.

Now, put your twenty-one pieces of paper into a bag. Then, taking care not to look, put your hand into the bag and draw out two names. So, for instance, your first two pieces might be Drin Hain and Slavious Doom – that means these two warriors will fight each other first! Before you conduct any battles, however, make sure you have drawn eight fights (i.e. sixteen pieces of paper). These eight battles represent the first 'round' of your tournament. The winner of each fight goes on to meet the winner of the next one, and so on – until only one gladiator remains! You can find the exact rules of combat over the page!

# HOW TO PLAY

The character with the lowest LP score goes first (if level, it's a coin toss), rolling two dice and adding them together for an 'attack' score. The defender also rolls two dice, for a 'defence' score. If the defence is higher than the attack, there is no damage, but if the attack is higher than the defence, the attacker rolls two dice AGAIN – and deducts the score from the defender's life points. Now, it is the defender's turn to attack. This goes on until one character has been reduced to zero.

Enjoy!

# LIFE POINTS

| | | | |
|---|---|---|---|
| Decimus Rex | 60 | Sturgenus | 30 |
| Slavious Doom | 60 | Tekaro | 40 |
| Olu | 20 | Miriki | 40 |
| Mirror Master | 30 | Aritezu | 40 |
| Ruma | 30 | Akina | 40 |
| Captain Lich | 20 | Mori | 10 |
| Teo | 20 | Falni | 10 |
| Drin Hain | 30 | Tiberius | 10 |
| Argon | 20 | Hrin | 10 |
| Groach | 50 | Boma Derok | 20 |
| Gladius | 30 | | |

# CHARACTER PROFILE
# THE MAW

**NAME:** Unknown (called the Maw)

**FROM:** The inky depths below Campania

**HEIGHT:** 6m approx

**WEIGHT:** 10 tons approx

**BODY TYPE:** Cephalopod

---

**Fact file:** The Maw is thought to be an ancient god of an elder race, left behind when the Earth was abandoned by the original deities who ruled it.

---

**THE MAW QUIZ:** How well do you know the Maw? Can you answer the following questions?

**1. DECIMUS WENT BACK TO THE MAW IN ORDER TO FETCH SOMETHING. WHAT WAS IT?**
**2. WHO WAS WITH DECIMUS WITH WHEN HE RETURNED TO THE CAVERN OF THE MAW?**
**3. WHAT IS IT THAT ARGON DOES TO CAUSE THE MAW GREAT DISTRESS?**

Answers: 1. The Blade of Fire 2. Argon 3. Yells/bellows.

# HOW MANY

# GLADIATOR
# BOY

## BOOKS DO
## YOU HAVE?

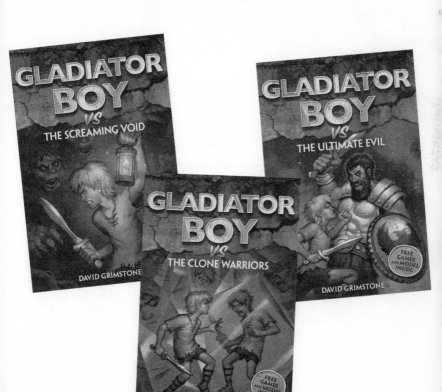

# GLADIATOR BOY

# WWW.GLADIATORBOY.COM

Have you checked out the Gladiator Boy website?
It's the place to go for games, downloads,
activities, sneak previews and lots of fun!

Sign up to the newsletter at
**WWW.GLADIATORBOY.COM**
and receive exclusive extra
content and the opportunity
to enter special members-only
competitions.